OTTER in Space

SAM GARTON

BALZER + BRAY
An Imprint of HarperCollins*Publishers*

This book is dedicated to Becca, best wife EVER!
(Who, coincidently, regards going to space as
the scariest thing imaginable.)
(Apart from spiders.)

Balzer + Bray is an imprint of HarperCollins Publishers. Otter in Space. For information address HarperCollins Children's Books, a division of HarperCollins Publishers, 195 Broadway, New York, NY 10007. www.harpercollinschildrens.com

ISBN 978-0-06-224776-6

The artist used Adobe Photoshop to create the digital illustrations for this book.
Typography by Dana Fritts
15 16 17 18 19 SCP 10 9 8 7 6 5 4 3 2 1
❖
First Edition

On Sunday, Otter Keeper took me and Teddy to the museum.
The museum is the best place ever!

We saw a huge
dinosaur skeleton

and met Teddy's cousin.

We also looked at old paintings,
made before crayons were invented.

In a museum, even boring things
become interesting if they are
old enough.

But our most favorite part was the special room all about outer space!

There were lots of fun things to do and buttons to press.

Teddy and I got to see a real moon rock. Otter Keeper said it came all the way from the moon.

And the moon is very far away. The video told us so.

Our last stop in the museum was a very important one: the gift shop!

Unfortunately, Otter Keeper said I couldn't buy everything I needed.

So I was forced to make some very difficult decisions.

On the way home, Teddy and I were a little sad.

We had a new spaceship, but we really needed a moon rock, too.

The next day, after Otter Keeper left for work, we were still sad. Playing in outer space was no fun with just a spaceship.

Teddy suggested going back to the museum to get a moon rock, but no one knew how to get there without Otter Keeper.

Giraffe offered to drive. But I don't think he really knows how.

I needed to think of a clever plan
to get my moon rock.

This took a long time.

Then suddenly, I had

the best idea ever!

Teddy and I would get our moon rock from the same place the museum did:

We made a very important list of very important things.

It was very important.

But before getting started, we decided to have our lunch.
Thinking of ideas and writing lists can make you hungry.

Lunch is very important, too.

The first thing on the list was to build our space suits. (You must not forget to bring a space suit if you're going to the moon.)

Unfortunately, our house has a lot of gravity . . .

and this can make it hard to properly test a space suit.

Teddy took his space suit off. He didn't seem to be taking space travel seriously.

So I decided it was time to start his training.

Problem solving wasn't his strong point.

But he impressed everyone with his performance in the antigravity training!

Teddy asked if Giraffe would be coming with us to the moon. I explained that Giraffe, of all people, certainly could *not* come.

Giraffe had a very important job back on Earth.

Now it was time to build our spaceship.

This was very important and I told everyone they had to help, but I still had to do most of the work myself.

Finally it was time for launch!

Lift-off went very well.

But we did have a bumpy moon landing.

And my space suit got
a little broken.

We didn't have long to find our moon rock, but luckily they were all hiding in the same place.

We chose the best moon rock we could find—the biggest one!

It was hard to get it back to Earth,
but Teddy and I agreed it was worth it.

The day got much better now that we had a moon rock to play with.

And then Otter Keeper came home.

We discovered he really doesn't like moon rocks. In fact, he was quite upset and said that the moon rock had to go back to where it came from.

This was a silly idea—we obviously couldn't get it back to the moon, because our spaceship was broken!

Otter Keeper said we could discuss what to do with the moon rock at dinner. I kept my space suit on the whole time, to show I was serious.

Finally Otter Keeper agreed to let us keep the
moon rock, but only if we took it outside for a bath.

That evening, Otter Keeper added "Do not dig up moon rocks" to our list of things not to do.

But he didn't say anything about digging up other things. So tomorrow, Teddy and I have decided to go back to the moon . . .

to dig up a dinosaur!